First published in Great Britain and the United States
in hardback in 1998
This edition published in 2000 by Zero to Ten Limited
327 High Street, Slough, Berkshire, SL1 1TX

Copyright © 2000 Zero to Ten Limited
Illustrations © 1998 Louise Batchelor

Publisher: Anna McQuinn
Art Director: Tim Foster
Senior Art Editor: Sarah Godwin

A CIP catalogue record for this book is available from the British Library.

ISBN: 1-84089-125-4

Printed in Hong Kong

Ding! Dong!

Illustrated by

Louise Batchelor

Hi!

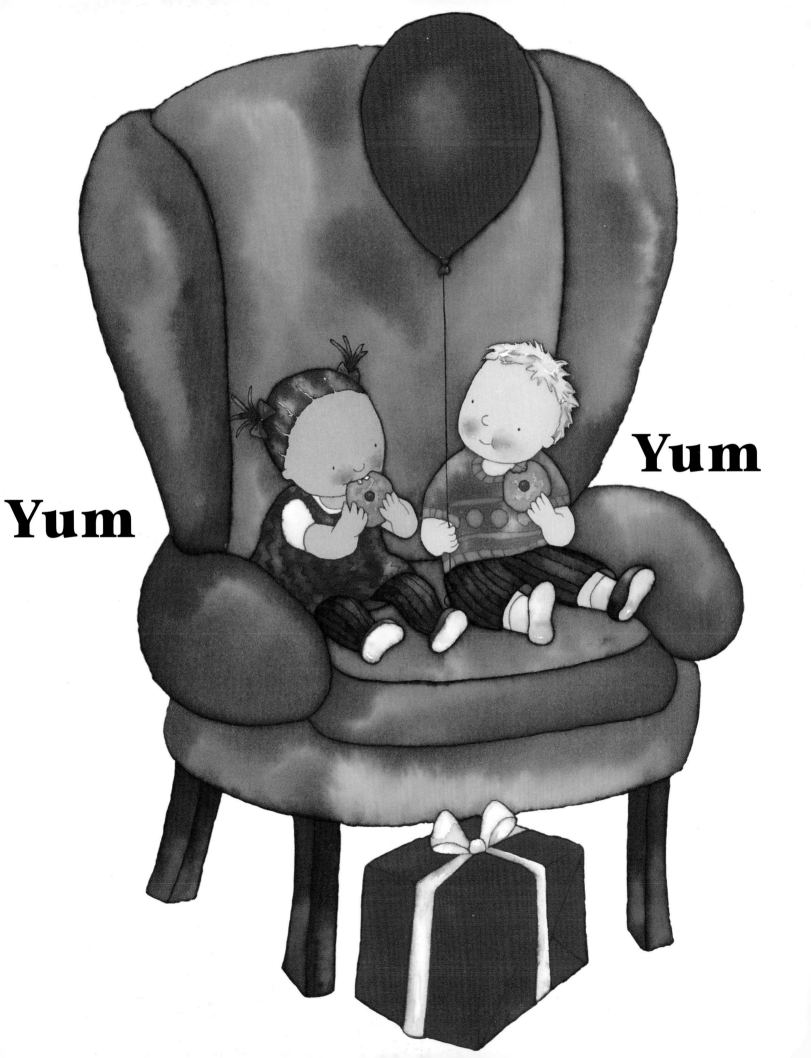

Yum

Yum

Thank you?

Thank you

Mine!

No!
Mine!

All gone

More!

Thank you

YUCK!

Bye-bye!

What the critics said about Whoops!

"Book of the Week, the indestructible Whoops!...
A major breakthrough; it's a full sized picture book
with a wonderfully clear story told in words
that even the smallest will recognise." *The Guardian*

"Large, sturdy pages showcase the ups and downs of a typical toddler play date,
from happy snacking to sharing dilemmas.
Minimal, expressive text in various size type and bright illustrations
perfectly capture the rhythms of first friendships
in a toddler friendly format." *The Horn Book*

"... a bold slice of toddler life..." *The Sunday Times*

"This book reinforces early speech by using many
of the first words and phrases babies learn...
a funny familiar story that babies and toddlers will love."
Junior Magazine

Other TODDLER BOOKS from ZERO TO TEN

More!

Swings! Come on! Push me! MORE!

On a walk in the park, two lively toddlers encounter ducks, a dog, swings...
Every parent and toddler will find the scenes immediately recognisable
and the simple story provides a perfect next step
from first word books.

The robust format is perfect for sharing –
you can use your child's name and tell your own story,
then enjoy the fun of saying the words aloud together!

ISBN: 1-84089-127-0

Uh-oh!

Don't worry. Look! Share! Squishy! Your friend!

This title follows our little girl's first day at nursery school,
from the tentative first moments through her growing confidence
until Dad picks her up at the end of the day.

ISBN: 1-84089-182-3